Granda

written by Pam Holden
illustrated by Samer Hatam

Is this one Grandad's home?
No, there is a skateboard
at this door.

It's not Grandad's skateboard!

Is this one Grandad's home?
No, there are running shoes
at this door.

Grandad can't go running!

Is this one Grandad's home?
No, there is a baseball bat
at this door.

Grandad can't play baseball.

Is this one Grandad's home?
No, there is a scooter at
this door.

It's not Grandad's scooter.

Is this one Grandad's home?
No, there is a soccer ball
at this door.

Grandad can't play soccer.

Is this Grandad's home?
No, there are skis at
this door.

They are not Grandad's skis.

Is this one Grandad's home?
No, there are slippers at
this door.

They are not Grandad's slippers!

This one is Grandad's home!
There is his fishing rod.
Yes, Grandad likes fishing!